CUDA OF THE CELTS

For Louis, Finlay and Alastair

S.A.

To Bentley and Morton Moss

R.L.

Adult supervision is recommended when sharp pointed items such as scissors are in use.

First published in Great Britain 2003
by Egmont Books Ltd
239 Kensington High Street, London W8 6SA

Paperback ISBN 1 4052 0613 6
10 9 8 7 6 5 4 3 2 1
A CIP catalogue record for this title is available from the British Library
Printed in U.A.E.

Go Bananas

1

IT WAS THE festival of Beltane. On a lonely farmstead in a corner of south-east Britain, the ritual fires had been lit, and Cuda and the other girls of her clan had decorated the trees with flowers. Cuda's clan was part of the Trinobantes tribe. This year, as well as to welcome the arrival of spring, the tribe had another reason to feast.

Outside the chieftain's roundhouse the women cooked in a great cauldron while the men squatted about the fire, painting blue patterns on their bodies. Bran, the bard, picked up his harp.

'Cuda, come here, my child,' he called.

Cuda ran to him. 'Yes, Father?'

'You know we ride to battle tomorrow?'

Cuda nodded eagerly. 'You're going to help the Iceni tribe avenge the terrible things the Romans did to Queen Boudicca.'

'That is so.' Softly Bran plucked a string. 'Tonight, after I have sung, you will sing in the way I taught you.'

'But, Father, can a girl sing on the eve of a battle?'

'Why not? The older girls are going to chant our war cries in front of the enemy. And if I don't return, you must know how to remind our women and children of their history and their heroes. Can you do that?'

Cuda raised her chin. 'I can, Father.'

Bran stroked her long red curls, which gleamed as brightly as the flames. 'Well done, my child. You are as brave as your mother was.'

'Can she see me from the Otherworld?' Cuda asked.

'Of course. And if I am sent there in this battle, she and I will both watch over you.'

Arn, the clan chieftain, rose to his feet. Dark blue scrolls and circles covered every inch of his chest. Round his neck a golden torque glinted, and his hair and his long moustache, which curled down below his chin, were dyed the colour of the sun.

'Listen, my people,' he said. 'The Romans, who have cruelly beaten the queen of the Iceni, are the same invaders who built a temple to their god on the fort of Camulos, our most sacred place. Tomorrow, we join the Iceni to win back Camulodun and drive the Romans from the shores of Britain for ever.'

The drinking horn was passed from hand to hand, and the warriors called for their bard.

Bran rose. First he chanted the names of all the past kings of the tribe. Then he sang a song about a hero who killed his enemy after a fight that lasted three days and three nights.

As the warriors cheered and asked for more, Bran held up his hand. 'Now my daughter will sing for you,' he said.

A hush fell as Cuda stepped forward. She wore a yellow tunic, and her amber necklace glittered and winked in the firelight.

'Sing, child,' Arn said, throwing back his head and swallowing a hornful of mead.

Cuda ran her fingers across the strings of her harp. Even though this was the first time she had sung for the clan, she was not afraid.

Starting softly, she sang of a goddess who could change into a tree or an animal. Her voice rose into the night as clear as the cry of a plover on the marshes. Even the hardy warriors wept.

Next morning, the clan was up before dawn. The women and children ran about bringing the men their long swords and shields, their tall spears and javelins, and their iron helmets. Bran held Cuda tightly to him.

'Be brave, daughter,' he whispered. 'You are now the tribe's memory. Whether in this world or in the Otherworld, we shall meet again.' Then, mounting his shaggy pony, Dubh, he galloped off after the war chariots.

2

THE MOON WANED. With the men gone, the women and children had to do all the work of the farm. Early every morning, Cuda got up from the pile of skins where she slept and went to feed the pigs and drive the sheep and cows into the meadows.

One morning, as she was milking a cow, resting her sleepy head against the animal's warm belly, she heard a wild shouting. The geese that patrolled the farm began to honk. Then a host of men, led by Bran, galloped into the farmstead.

'Father, what's happened?' Cuda cried, rushing to hold Dubh's halter.

Leaping down, Bran hugged her. 'A great victory, Cuda. As we reached Camulodun, the Roman statue fell on its face. No one knows how it happened, but we knew it meant the gods were with us.'

As the women rushed out to greet the warriors, Cuda went to help her father wash off his battle stains.

'Father, did the Romans all run away?' she asked.

'No, child. We killed them.'

'All of them? Even the children?'

'It was as the gods wanted.'

'But did you kill them?'

Shaking the drops of water off his hair, Bran bent and put his hands on his daughter's shoulders. 'When the Romans came to our land many seasons ago,' he told her, 'our king made a pact with them and, after a time, they went away. But when I was a boy, they returned with many legions. They took our lands and carried our people off to be slaves. Now, we must drive them out. But' – and here he lifted her chin with his finger and looked into her eyes – 'the Romans too are people, and I would never kill a child.'

That night all the nearby clans gathered in a sacred grove to celebrate the victory. Decked in their finest clothes and jewellery, the people chanted and danced. A bull was led forward. Calling on the gods to accept the beast as an offering, a Druid cut its throat with his knife.

Again Bran and the warriors rode off to battle. The next morning, Cuda went to fetch water from a spring in the woods. As she bent to fill her bucket, she glimpsed a terrified face peering at her from the undergrowth. Cuda froze; her heart raced. Then a boy staggered out and collapsed at her feet. He wore a Roman tunic and cloak, and she saw that one of his legs oozed blood.

Her fear vanished. Tearing a strip of cloth from her tunic, Cuda tried to remember the Latin words her father had taught her.

'Are you Roman?' she asked, as she bathed the boy's wound.

He clenched his teeth in pain and nodded.

'Camulodun?' Cuda asked. 'From the battle?'

A look of terror crossed the boy's face, but again he nodded.

'Cuda,' the girl said, pointing to herself. Then she pointed at him.

'Marcus,' said the boy, adding something quickly in Latin. When he saw that Cuda did not understand, he made signs to explain what he was saying.

Bit by bit, Cuda understood that all Marcus's family had been killed except his father, who had been away from home.

'Come,' Cuda said. Helping the boy up, she half carried him to an abandoned foxhole and signed to him to wriggle down into it. Then she covered his head with branches.

At supper, as the clan sat round the fire discussing the great battle, Cuda snatched a piece of meat from the cauldron and crept off into the wood.

It was pitch dark. She had to feel her way to the foxhole. 'Marcus?' she whispered.

There was no reply. Pushing some of the branches aside, Cuda felt the boy's face. It was warm. He was alive.

'Eat,' she said, putting the piece of meat in his hand.

Ravenous, Marcus wolfed the food. He wanted to climb out of the hole, but Cuda whispered, 'No, no,' and, groping for Marcus's hand, she drew his finger across her throat to show him what would happen if he were found.

Back at the fire, Cuda sang for the clan. Afterwards, as she lay listening to the howl of wolves and the snorting of wild boar in the woods, she thought of the boy alone in the dark and of what would happen if her people found out that she had helped him. For his sake and her own, she had to be strong.

Soon Marcus was better. Now when Cuda came, he tried to amuse her by imitating the animals he saw around him in the forest.

'A badger?' Cuda guessed, as he snuffled and grunted at the food she had smuggled to him.

'Bad-ger,' Marcus repeated.

The two children stifled their giggles.

Then one evening, as Cuda knelt beside the foxhole, Marcus suddenly grabbed her arm.

'Look!' he whispered. Turning, Cuda saw Anu, a girl from the clan, running out of the wood.

'Go,' Cuda told Marcus. 'Run fast.'

There was no time to say goodbye. Wriggling out of the hole, Marcus vanished into the undergrowth.

Moments after, the whole clan burst through the bushes. 'Where is the Roman boy?' one cried.

'Why are you hiding him?' demanded another.

'Show us where he is, Cuda.'

Frightened, but knowing that Marcus's life depended on her, Cuda faced her angry people.

'There is no boy,' she said. 'If Anu had looked closer, she would have seen he was a spirit who came out of the spring from Annwn, the Otherworld.'

3

MONTHS PASSED, AND news came that the tribes had sacked the Roman towns of Londinium and Verulamium. At the farmstead, the women and children mowed the hay and harvested the grain. As the days grew shorter, they began to prepare for Sammain, the great festival of the beginning of the year, when spirits walked the earth and cattle would be sacrificed to the gods.

One afternoon, Cuda and another girl were guarding the geese in a distant meadow, when they saw a dark pall of smoke rising from a nearby village. Then two boys ran up.

'The tribes have been defeated,' one of them gasped. 'Our warriors are all dead or captured. The Romans have burned our village and taken our people away to be slaves.'

'Where are you going?' Cuda cried. But the boys had disappeared into the woods.

When the girls got back to the farm, all was in uproar. Babies screamed, horses neighed in terror. Some of the women grabbed their children and ran towards the marshes. Others seized weapons and fled for the woods. Finding herself alone, Cuda ran to the spring where she had met Marcus and wriggled down into the foxhole.

'Goddess Nemotona, protect me,' she begged. 'Bran, my father, and my mother look up from the Otherworld and take care of me.'

She could hear men crashing through the thicket, shouting to each other. A sword slashed close by.

Then a hand grasped her shoulder, and she was jerked out of the hole. Bloodshot eyes glared into hers.

'It's a girl,' the soldier bawled, drawing his sword.

As Cuda shrank away in terror, a centurion strode over and seized her. 'Girl slaves are worth money,' he said.

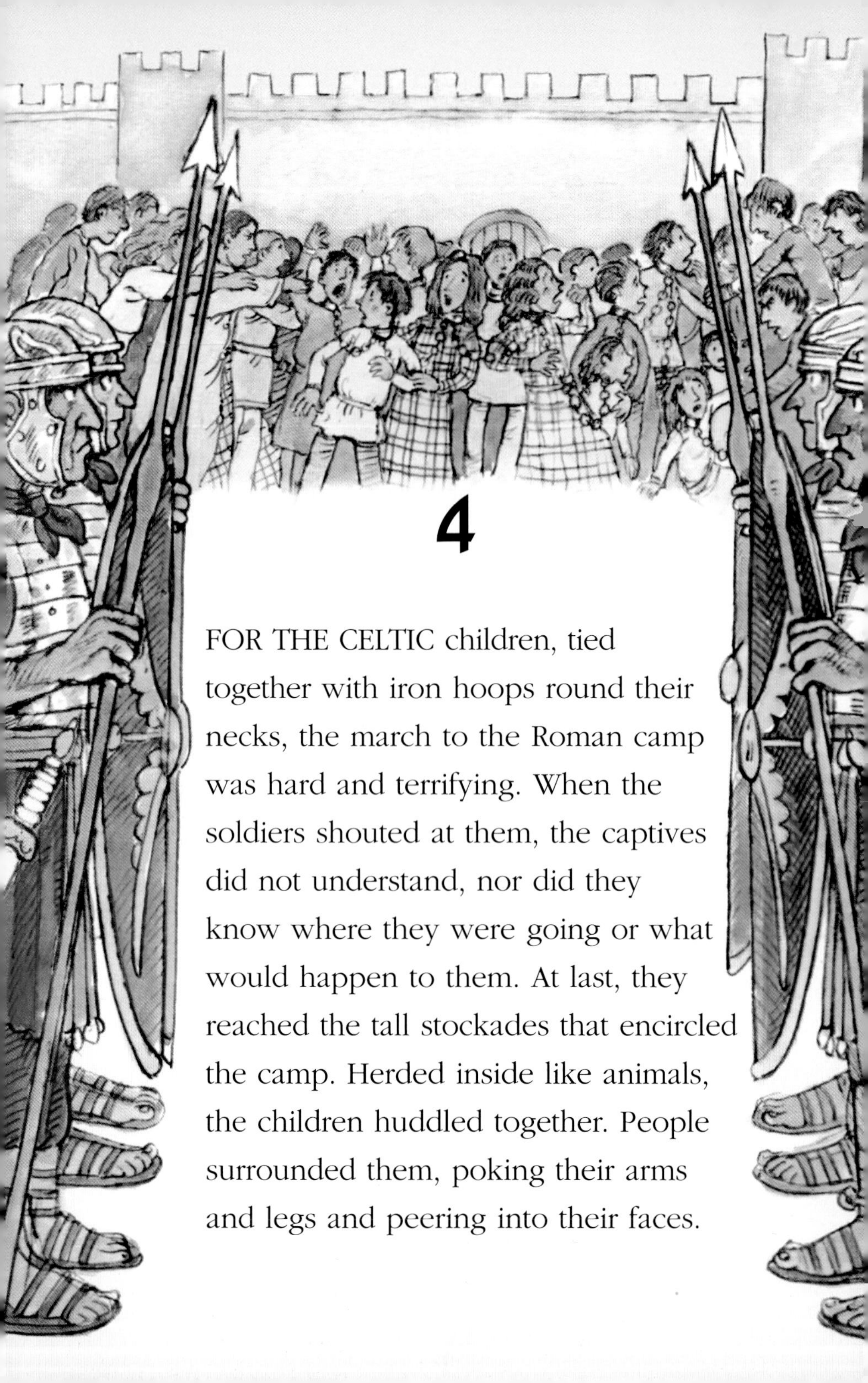

4

FOR THE CELTIC children, tied together with iron hoops round their necks, the march to the Roman camp was hard and terrifying. When the soldiers shouted at them, the captives did not understand, nor did they know where they were going or what would happen to them. At last, they reached the tall stockades that encircled the camp. Herded inside like animals, the children huddled together. People surrounded them, poking their arms and legs and peering into their faces.

'They're going to kill us,' a girl whimpered.

'To die is better than to be a slave,' said an older boy. 'We must show them we are not afraid.'

A fat man in a greasy tunic and leather apron seized Cuda by the arm. Bawling to one of the soldiers, he held out a coin.

Just then a fanfare of trumpets sounded. Everyone drew back as a column of Roman infantry tramped in through the gates. They wore helmets and armour. Swords hung at their belts, and they carried tall spears and huge curved shields. When their centurion shouted, they all stopped at the same time. The children had never before seen such a sight. No one ever told a British warrior on his war chariot what to do. Each man and his charioteer fought for themselves.

The merchant tightened his grip on Cuda's arm, but the centurion called out again, and now the ranks of soldiers drew aside. Four men came forward, carrying a litter on their shoulders. They lowered it, and a stern-faced man in a white toga climbed down.

'Hail!' he said, raising his arm.

Every legionary raised an arm in salute.

'Hail to the lord procurator!' they cried.

All at once, a small figure on a white pony rode out of the retinue that followed the litter. Jumping off his horse, he saluted the procurator and then he pointed straight at Cuda. The girl gasped. The boy was Marcus.

The centurion snatched Cuda from the fat merchant and led her in front of the stern-faced man.

'Tell the procurator your name, girl,' the soldier said in Cuda's language.

The iron hoop round Cuda's neck bit into her flesh. Her whole body ached with exhaustion. But she raised her head proudly.

'I am Cuda of the Trinobantes,' she replied.

The procurator spoke to Marcus, who answered in a long sentence.

'The son of the lord procurator says you saved his life,' the centurion translated.

'He also says you have the voice of a skylark and can charm the angry gods with your singing. Is this true?'

'My people say so,' Cuda told him.

The procurator's stern face broke into a smile. Then he gave an order to one of the mounted soldiers, who leaned down and lifted Cuda on to his horse. Marcus too mounted his pony. Then the procurator climbed back on to his litter and, with Cuda on the soldier's pommel and Marcus riding alongside, the whole retinue set off out of the camp.

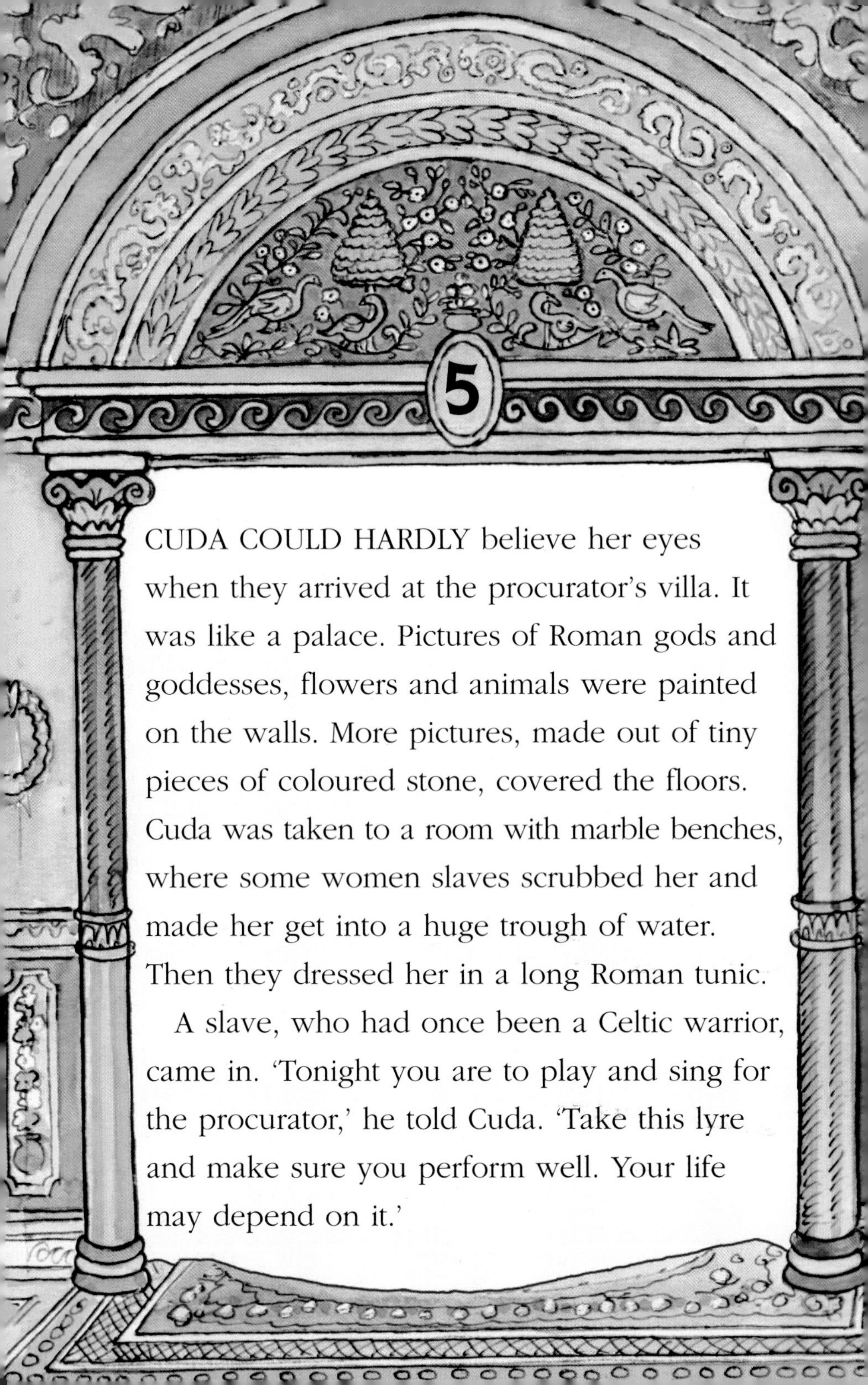

5

CUDA COULD HARDLY believe her eyes when they arrived at the procurator's villa. It was like a palace. Pictures of Roman gods and goddesses, flowers and animals were painted on the walls. More pictures, made out of tiny pieces of coloured stone, covered the floors. Cuda was taken to a room with marble benches, where some women slaves scrubbed her and made her get into a huge trough of water. Then they dressed her in a long Roman tunic.

A slave, who had once been a Celtic warrior, came in. 'Tonight you are to play and sing for the procurator,' he told Cuda. 'Take this lyre and make sure you perform well. Your life may depend on it.'

Cuda had never seen a lyre before, but it looked a bit like her harp. Holding it under her arm, she tried a few notes. The lyre sang. Softly, stopping now and again to correct herself, Cuda began to play one of her tribe's old songs.

At last, the slave came back and led her into a huge hall, where men in togas reclined on benches. Firebrands flickered on the walls, and slaves hurried by with jugs of wine and platters of meat and fruit. No one took any notice of Cuda.

'Play,' the slave said in a low voice.

Nervous now that she was singing for her life, Cuda could not utter a word.

'Sing,' said the slave more harshly.

'What shall I sing?' Cuda whispered.

'Cuda,' called a voice. To the girl's joy, Marcus stepped out of the shadows. Flashing her a smile, he spoke to the slave.

'The procurator's son says sing as you did for your clan when he was hiding in the foxhole,' the slave told her. 'He will stand beside you and protect you.'

With Marcus there, Cuda felt strong and she lifted up her voice and sang. The men in togas stopped talking and listened.

At last the procurator spoke to the slave.

'My lord says you are to be freed and to live in his household,' the slave told Cuda.

Marcus took her hand. 'You will be my sister, Cuda,' he said, 'and I shall teach you my language.'

Two moons came and went. For Cuda, life at the villa was much easier than at the farmstead. Instead of working all day in the fields, she learned to read and write the Latin language. When the weather grew cold, fires were lit under the floors and the whole house stayed warm. But Cuda did not forget her people.

One winter's day, as the children sat playing a game with a dice and a board, Marcus said, 'You're thinking about your clan, aren't you, Cuda?'

The girl nodded. 'I wish I knew what had happened to them. And, more than anything, to my father.'

Marcus put his arm round her shoulders. 'My mother and brother died, so I understand. I'll ask my father if he can help. His own grandfather was a Celt, and he hates to see the Celtic people cruelly treated.'

A few days later, Marcus came bounding into the room where Cuda was studying.

'The hoops are to be struck from the necks of the British women and children,' he told her. 'They are to be set free and sent home. My father has decreed it.'

'Home? Oh, Marcus!'

'If you could, would you go with them?' Marcus asked, suddenly anxious.

Cuda hesitated. Then, flinging her arms round him, she said, 'This is my home now, and you're my brother.'

That spring, work began on the rebuilding of the forum in Camulodun. One day, the children saw a line of slaves trudging by on their way to a stone quarry. One of them was grey-haired and covered in sores. Overjoyed but horrified, Cuda recognised Bran.

In tears, she turned to Marcus. 'That man is my father, the finest bard of our tribe,' she said. 'Help him or he will die.'

Marcus grabbed her hand. 'Come on. I know what to do.'

The two children ran back to the villa, and Marcus told his father of the terrible fate of Bran, the bard.

The procurator thought for a while. Then he said, 'I shall see if he can be found.'

It was Marcus's birthday. First, he and Cuda went to the shrine of Minerva and laid gifts on the altar. Then they returned home for the party. All the important Romans had been invited.

As the guests dined, musicians in strange costumes played pipes, and girls and boys danced. Acrobats leaped and somersaulted, and jugglers threw clubs into the air. Then, just as Marcus rose to his feet to thank his guests for honouring his birthday, a commotion broke out. A grey-haired man limped into the hall. The guards went to seize him, but the procurator held up his hand.

'Let him enter,' he commanded.

The man raised his head, and Cuda saw that it was Bran. Almost at the same time, Bran saw her. Joyfully, he threw away his staff and took a lyre from the hands of a musician.

'I sing to Marcus, the Roman, and to Cuda, the Celt,' he cried. Then he plucked the lyre, and his voice rang out as he told of how, through the children, peace and friendship came between the Trinobantes and the Romans.

THE CELTS AND THE ROMANS

IN AD 43, the Romans invaded Britain. They came from a city in Italy called Rome, in search of land and wealth. The Roman army were terrified of going to Britain because they had heard about the fierce Celts who lived there.

DID YOU KNOW?
The Romans called Britain, Britannia.

THE CELTS LIVED in small groups or tribes, each ruled by a chief. The tribes often fought one another, so when the Romans invaded, some tribes decided to support them, while others fought against them in fierce battles.

Gradually, the Romans gained more and more control over Britain. Celtic leaders, like Queen Boudicca led revolts against the Romans, but they were defeated.

For nearly 300 years after the Celtic rebellions, the people of Britain lived peaceful. The Romans were good rulers. They built roads and big towns, and made sensible laws. They also introduced new religions and methods of farming. People enjoyed living in Roman-style towns with public baths and shops.

Sites and artefacts from Roman times still survive. Archeologists study them to discover more about how the ancient Romans lived their daily lives.

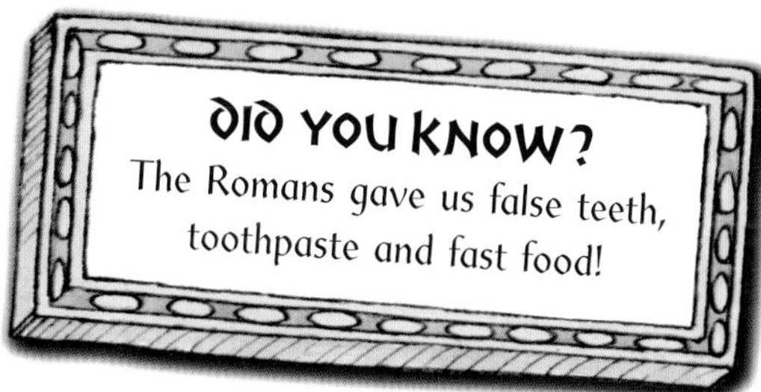

I LIVE WITH my father in a small settlement. We live in a house with a thatched roof called a roundhouse. Father grows crops such as wheat and barley, and keeps sheep, cattle and some pigs. I help him in the fields to look after the animals. There is always much to do.

IN MY TRIBE, there are many skilled craftspeople. They make useful objects like tools and pottery. We trade goods with other tribes from all over Britain and other countries.

I LIVE WITH my father in a large Roman town. He helps govern the country. He has an important job, so we have slaves to help us. We live in a house called a villa. In many rooms, there are large colourful mosaics made from tiny pieces of stone.

I DON'T GO to school, but I study at home with a tutor. I learn reading, writing and maths. I also have to learn Latin and Greek. In my free time, I like to play board games and go to the theatre to see plays.

CUDA AND MARCUS have very different lives. How are they different? Imagine you live in a roundhouse or in a villa, and write about your day. Try and describe your home.

1=I
2=II
3=III
4=IV
5=V
6=VI
7=VII
8=VIII
9=IX
10=X
'I have to learn counting from one to ten using Roman numerals.'
XII I II III IIII V VI VII VIII IX X XI
ROMAN NUMERALS ARE still used today. Look around and see where you can spot them.
WHAT YOU WILL NEED:
1 large piece of white sugar paper or thin card.
1 pen or pencil.
1 pair of scissors.
Some crayons or felt tips.
1. Think of your favourite number. Work out what that would be in roman numerals. Carefully draw it on your paper, then ask an adult to cut it out.
2. Now decorate the number. Why not try colouring it in in a Roman style, like a mosaic?